B55 065 303 6

Maverick

Chapter Readers

'Secret Spaniel'
An original concept by Lou Treleaven
© Lou Treleaven

Illustrated by Antonella Fant

Published by MAVERICK ARTS PUBLISHING LTD
Studio 11, City Business Centre, 6 Brighton Road,
Horsham, West Sussex, RH13 5BB
© Maverick Arts Publishing Limited November 2020
+44 (0)1403 256941

A CIP catalogue record for this book is available at the British Library.

ISBN 978-1-84886-733-8

Maverick
publishing
www.maverickbooks.co.uk

Grey

This book is rated as: Grey Band (Guided Reading)

Secret Spaniel

To the real Maddy and Hammy,
with fond memories.

Written by
Lou Treleaven

Illustrated by
Antonella Fant

Chapter 1

"Maddy! Over here!" Brutus the Boxer dog was talking to me. I wandered away from where my owner was standing, to find out what he wanted.

"I hear you're good at finding things and solving problems," Brutus said. "They call you 'The Nose'. When you found that missing pup, it even got into the papers."

I wagged my tail. It was nice to be famous!

"I need your help," said Brutus. "I've got problems."

I looked at him. "What problems?" I asked.

"It's the Dog Show. The one at the Village Fete. I've won that show twice—and I could win it again this year." Brutus edged closer. "But they say some out-of-town

hound is going to steal the show."

"So another dog might win. Big deal," I said. Every dog in the village had imagined winning the Dog Show at some point. Even I'd pictured myself with a gorgeous red rosette.

As if that could ever happen after last time.

"But this isn't a village dog. I've heard this dog is from London," Brutus growled. "There's no way I'm going to lose to a dog from London. So you have to help me, Maddy. I need to find out who the mystery dog is."

"And then what?" I asked.

Brutus's hackles rose. "We take action."

I didn't like the way he was talking. But maybe this mystery dog was a local one after all. If I could find that out, Brutus wouldn't need to take his 'action', whatever that meant.

"Okay, I'll do it," I said. "But if it turns out to be a local dog, you have to promise you'll back off."

Brutus wagged his tail. "They don't call you 'The Nose'

for nothing."

"They don't call me 'The Nose' at all," I pointed out. But it wasn't a bad nickname. I did have a pretty nose.

We walked back to our humans. Mike was telling Brutus's owner all about the engine he was restoring for his model railway. He hadn't noticed her yawning. I dragged him away. Poor Mike.

Chapter 2

When I got home, Hamlet the cat was waiting for me.

"I know what you're doing," he smirked. "You're trying to find out who the mystery dog is—the one who's going to enter the show. Archibald overheard the gossip at the dog toilet."

"That old fleabag," I said, hunching over Mike's notebook with a pen in my paw.

"You'll never work it out. Finding that missing puppy was a fluke."

"You're just jealous because you've never been in the newspaper."

Hamlet ignored me, hooked his claws around the door of the tumble drier and began dragging clothes into a basket. Hamlet was not your usual cat.

And I was not your usual dog.

Mike was brilliant at his job (designing fancy logos) but the clumsiest human ever. We did as much as we could to help. He thought he had a cleaning lady who he never saw. Only we knew the truth: 'Mrs Goodboys' wasn't real and her name came from a tin of dog food.

"Don't you want to know what Archibald said?" Hamlet purred, folding a t-shirt.

"Okay, what did Archibald say?"

"The Village Fete Committee is meeting at the café tomorrow to discuss an important guest who's entering the Dog Show."

"The café? I'll be there!" I raised an ear as a key turned in the lock. "Mike's coming! Get ready!"

Hamlet curled up on the laundry. I shoved the vacuum cleaner into the cupboard and raced up the hall.

Mike tickled my ears and I led him into the utility room for my tea. But he was distracted by the sight of Hamlet on his favourite t-shirt.

"Bad Hamlet! What would Mrs Goodboys say?"

If only Mike knew who really did his washing.

Chapter 3

The next day, I sneaked out to the café, Gazza's Grub. The lunchtime customers were sitting outside enjoying the sunshine.

"Fancy a cuppa?" Gazza's dog, Scruffy, said with a friendly sniff.

"Sorry. Here on business."

"Don't expect me to pick it up."

"Not that sort of business. I need to eavesdrop on the Village Fete Committee."

Scruffy nodded. "Follow me," he said, leading me to a shady spot.

"Great news!" one of the committee was saying.

"Tamsin Parker-Smetherington has agreed to open the fete! She's on the cover of *Pampered Pooches*. Doesn't Sweetikins look adorable? She'll steal the show."

Sweetikins! Brutus was right, a celebrity dog *was* going to steal the show!

The committee members forgot to take the magazine with them—which meant I could sneak it home. I raced back and pored over it.

'*Miss Tamsin Parker-Smetherington and Sweetikins attend the premiere of the new Jane Bond movie.*' The photograph showed a young woman in red carrying a tiny dog in a handbag.

I imagined Mike carrying me in a handbag. He would break his back.

"Some of us have better things to do than flick through magazines," Hamlet said, pushing a floor mop into the cupboard.

"I'm working on a case."

Hamlet stalked over. "No self-respecting cat would answer to the name of Sweetikins."

I was about to say cats were too stupid to answer to any name when I remembered it was Thursday—bathroom day. Hamlet was always tetchy after de-clogging the toilet. I turned back to the magazine.

'Tamsin will be in London on Friday at Cobblestones Bookshop, where Sweetikins will be signing copies of her autobiography, Dog Star.'

That was tomorrow! If I could meet Sweetikins at the bookshop, I could persuade her not to enter the show. All I had to do was get to the station, get on a train, go to London, find the bookshop, persuade Sweetikins and come home. Easy.

I lay down in my basket, my brain spinning.

Chapter 4

The next day, I ate my breakfast double-quick and ran to the garage. When Mike came in, ready for work, I was already hiding in the back of the car. He started the engine and we were off.

At the station car park, I jumped out while Mike paid for a ticket, then followed him to the platform and hid behind a bin. Mike's train arrived with a roar. I leapt on behind him and crawled under a seat.

There was a nice rocking motion. I was half-asleep when we reached King's Cross Station in London. I followed Mike out of the station.

Cars honked and big red buses filled the road. Huge

buildings loomed over pavements packed with people. Mike disappeared. His smell was gone too, lost in a tangle of scents.

I ran towards the road and a bus blasted its horn. London was much bigger than the village. I walked for miles, getting more and more lost. When I saw a bowl of water in a shop doorway, I rushed over and started lapping.

"What are you playing at, man?" A greying, bearded Jack Russell sat next to an old man, asleep in a pile of blankets. On the dish was the name 'Merlin'.

"Sorry," I said. "I was so thirsty I couldn't stop myself."

"You look dead on your paws. Have a good slurp. So what's up, man? Lost?"

I explained that I was trying to find Cobblestones Bookshop to see Sweetikins.

"Not in my patch. But then we don't go far. Tell you what, see those cardboard boxes? Tear off a piece. Now,

next to my owner there's a pen."

I did as he said, then gave them to Merlin who began to write. Another dog who could write just like me! I wondered if he secretly helped his owner too.

"This should do it," Merlin said, handing me the sign he'd written. "One more thing. See that hamburger box?"

I bounded off and retrieved it.

"Been hankering after that all day," he said between mouthfuls. "You're cool, man. Lady. You're a cool lady, man."

We sniffed goodbye, and I read a sign by Merlin's owner.

COLLECTING NEW WHEELS FOR MERLIN – BACK LEGS PARALYSED.

So Merlin couldn't walk. Well, I hoped he enjoyed his burger.

Chapter 5

On the sign, Merlin had written, '*If lost, please return to Cobblestones Bookshop*'. I sat on a corner, looking hopeful. Soon a nice couple put me in a taxi.

"We're going there too," the lady said.

I wondered if Merlin had ever used the same trick himself.

The bookshop windows were plastered with posters of Tamsin and Sweetikins. The queue to get in was enormous. A manager came out to say Tamsin would be ready in five minutes.

I slipped inside. The bookshop was a calm, quiet place with shelves of books. Tamsin sat at a table, wagging her finger at a Yorkshire Terrier in a frilly tutu.

"You'll just *have* to get ink on your paws, Sweety. How else will you sign your booky-wooks?"

Sweetikins yapped and dived under the table. I darted over before Tamsin could notice.

"Having trouble?" I asked Sweetikins.

"I am *not* putting my paw into a blob of ink!" Sweetikins sniffed.

"I could teach you how to sign your name instead," I offered.

Sweetikins narrowed her eyes. "Who are you and what do you want?" she asked me. "Are you a stalker?"

"No, I'm a Springer Spaniel. My name's Maddy and I'm here to ask you not to enter the Village Dog Show." I told Sweetikins all about Brutus, the show and how important it was to the other dogs that a village dog should win it.

"But I'm supposed to turn up at things. I have a book to promote," said Sweetikins.

"Yes—how exactly *did* you write a book?"

"Ghost writer," Sweetikins sniffed. "That means somebody writes the book for you. You know nothing about being a celebrity, do you? Never mind. Now, how do I do this writing thing?"

I told Sweetikins to get a pen and paper off the table and showed her how to grip the pen to make some basic letter shapes. It would have to do.

"Come to Mummy, you naughty darling," Tamsin called to Sweetikins.

"Now that I've helped you, will you help me by not

coming to the show?" I asked.

"I'll do what I can," Sweetikins said. "And thanks. You're not bad—for a non-celeb."

I gave her a goodbye lick. She disappeared into Tamsin's arms. I had to spit on the carpet: she was wearing perfume!

It tasted like washing-up liquid.

Chapter 6

I sat next to the nice couple I had met earlier to watch the book signing, then followed the crowd as they left. Most people headed for the nearest tube station so I jumped on with them. When I heard a voice say 'King's Cross', I slipped off and followed the flow of people.

"You're supposed to carry dogs on the escalator," a woman said, glaring at the man behind her as we glided towards the main station.

"I haven't got a dog..." I heard him say

as I trotted off.

There were so many people. How would I find Mike? If I missed him, I could be stranded in London! I'd be a stray, like Hamlet's mangy friend Archibald, only better looking.

After a long wait, I caught a whiff of Mike. His trail was weak amongst the crowd but I followed it to the ticket barrier. I jumped on the train just before the doors closed, wriggled through some legs and dived under a seat, heart thumping.

I crawled along under the seats until I found Mike. He had a big shopping bag on the floor. I clambered into it and covered myself with frozen meals as the passengers stared into newspapers and phones. Shivering, I waited until the doors slid open.

"Oof," Mike exclaimed as he hoisted the bag—and me— out of the train. I had been wondering what it would be like to have Mike carry me around in a handbag. Now I knew. It was a terrible experience. For both of us.

Chapter 7

I had done all I could. Now I just wanted to avoid Brutus, but Mike had other ideas. We had come to the hills for a walk and Mike headed straight towards Brutus's owner to give her the update on his engine renovation. He hadn't noticed her yawning after all.

"Your plan didn't work," Brutus snarled.

"Oh?" I said, trying to wander away.

"Haven't you seen the posters? That celebrity dog is going to steal the show." Brutus let out a low growl. "It's time for action. Sweetikins, or whatever she's called, will wish she'd never set paw in this village."

"No!" I yelped. "Let me speak to her. I'll get her to change her mind."

"Too late. You've had your chance. And I'm not calling you 'The Nose' anymore." Brutus bared his teeth.

After all my efforts, things were even worse.

★★★

That evening, Mike, Hamlet and I relaxed as Mike set up his favourite train set. When Mike left the room to get snacks, my thoughts turned back to the Dog Show.

"The only way to sort out this mess is to enter the show myself," I said.

Hamlet's ears pricked up. "You swore you would never enter again!"

"I went to all that trouble to meet Sweetikins. I don't want anything bad to happen to her."

I had to convince Mike to enter me, and it wasn't going to be easy. Not after what had happened last time.

Three years ago, I had won the 'Dog With The Most Beautiful Eyes' and had gone on to compete for 'Best in Show'. As Mike led me around, I showed off my glossy coat and wet nose for all I was worth.

The judge came over and stroked me, saying how beautiful I was. I felt sure I would win.

Then, in his nervousness, Mike dropped my lead. He stooped down, but stood up too quickly. Crack! Mike's head crashed into the judge's face.

"My nose!" the judge gasped. The cup shot out of her hands and flew through the air.

"I've got it!" Mike cried.

He dived. He fell. He landed on the cup.

Crunch! The cup was a crumpled mess.

We had never dared enter the Dog Show again.

✷✷✷

My cunning plan, when I finally thought of one, was so cunning I could hardly believe it might work. But it had to. I asked Hamlet to write a letter.

"It's good practice for you," I told Hamlet as he struggled to grip the biro. "Add a kiss."

"He'll never believe that."

"Don't you want to make Mike happy?"

Hamlet groaned. "There."

I placed the letter on the front doormat.

Dear Mike,
Please enter Maddy in the Dog Show. It would be so lovely for

Brutus and me to see you there.
I like toy trains too. They are fun
to chase.

Brutus's human

X

PS You smell nice and have lovely
silky ears.

When Mike got home that night, he was so delighted
that I felt a tiny bit guilty for tricking him. But only a bit.
Because my plan worked—we were going to the Dog
Show!

Chapter 8

It was the day of the fete. The air smelt of cut grass and sizzling bacon as Mike and I walked to the school field. I had been washed and brushed until I gleamed. The plan was going perfectly. I would talk to Sweetikins, sort everything out, and then maybe there would even be a rosette and a hog roast.

I pulled Mike over to the judge's tent to book us in.

"Maddy, isn't it?" the judge said, looking at Mike with a pained expression. There was still a scar on her nose.

Mike turned red and filled in our entry slip. As we hurried away, a pink limousine pulled up. Out stepped Tamsin in a pink jumpsuit with Sweetikins riding in her handbag.

"Wow, is that Tamsin Parker-Smethy-thingy—" Mike began.

I dragged him towards the drinks tent. If he saw too much of Tamsin he would go to pieces.

"Alright, Maddy?" said a familiar voice. "Gazza's entered me for the Dog Show." It was Scruffy from the café. He nodded at Gazza, a shaggy-haired man with a half tucked-in shirt and trailing shoelaces. "We're in the 'Dog Most Like Its Owner' class."

"Good choice," I said. "Keep Mike busy, will you? I'll be back for the show."

I followed the smell of perfume to the hall. Tamsin was signing autographs. Sweetikins was curled up in her handbag under the table.

I skidded to a halt beside Sweetikins. "You agreed not to come!"

"I never agreed to anything," Sweetikins yawned.

"But you don't understand—" I began.

"Too right she doesn't!" snarled Brutus. "You're

coming with me, little lady."

"My name is Sweetikins Deliciousness Cutiepie the Third," Sweetikins said haughtily, "and I'm not leaving this bag."

"Suits me," Brutus said, grabbing the handle with his teeth. I grabbed the other end, but Brutus was too strong. Soon I was sliding along like a water skier. I had to let go before I lost my teeth.

"Wait!" I barked. "I'm coming with you. Let's talk about this."

I ran after Brutus as he pulled the yapping Sweetikins into a store room. Everyone had been too busy admiring Tamsin to notice a thing.

"Here's where it stops. Time to talk," I said.

"You two talk. I've got a show to win." Brutus bounded to the door with an evil grin.

"No!" I barked.

With a final flash of his teeth, Brutus leapt out and closed the door. Before I could spring to the handle, a scraping noise told me Brutus was dragging a heavy table across the door.

We were trapped!

Chapter 9

I scrabbled against the door but it was wedged shut. The only other exit was a small, high window. "We're trapped!" I yelped.

"Perhaps I'll catch up on my beauty sleep. You can..." Sweetikins glanced up at a shelf of stationery. "Write a novel or something."

"But Tamsin will be worried! Don't you care?" I said, thinking of Mike in the beer tent.

"I'm sure she'll send one of her assistants to look for me." Sweetikins curled up in her bag.

I sat down. "It'll be too late by then."

"Too late for what?"

"The Dog Show. I wanted—I mean, *you* wanted to enter, didn't you?"

"We're here to *judge* 'Best in Show'. You think I'd parade around a car park?" Sweetikins closed her eyes. "I've competed at Crufts."

"So why didn't you tell Brutus you weren't entering?"

"I wasn't going to give that bully the satisfaction of thinking he could tell *me* what to do. Who does he think he is?"

"Last year's winner, that's who," I sighed. "Oh Sweetikins. If you'd told Brutus this before, we wouldn't be stuck in here now."

"Never mind. Tamsin will send someone. In the meantime, we might as well have a nap. It helps the time to pass."

"Perhaps you're right." I slumped down and laid my head on my paws. "I probably wouldn't have had a chance in the show anyway." I closed my eyes and tried not to think about Mike worrying. He was used to me roaming about, but once the Dog Show started he would be looking for me. Not turning up felt like I was letting him down.

"*You* were going to enter the show?" Sweetikins said.

"Only so I could keep an eye on you. I'd never win, anyway."

"Don't be silly! What time does the show start?"

"Any minute. But there's no way out. Anyway, you said Tamsin will find us."

"We can't wait until then." Sweetikins jumped up. "You want to enter the show, I'll get you to the show. Sweetikins always gets what she wants."

Sweetikins clambered up the shelves towards the window. "This pane is loose," she puffed, giving it a push.

"Can I help?"

"No need. There are some good things about being small. Here goes."

I heard a yelp as the windowpane fell outwards and Sweetikins tumbled out after it.

There was a crash and a thump.

"Sweetikins! Are you hurt?"

I heard one answering bark, then nothing.

I sat by the door for what seemed like ages. Then I heard a scraping noise. Sweetikins rushed in, followed by a huge man in a suit and sunglasses.

"Tamsin's bodyguard," Sweetikins said. "He'll make sure you get to the Dog Show safely."

I gaped up at the enormous man and then back at Sweetikins. "You're not just a pretty face after all!"

"Of course not," she said.

"Talking of pretty faces, we've got about one minute to get you ready for the show." Sweetikins scurried to Tamsin's handbag. "My own range of grooming products," she explained, selecting a heart-shaped brush. "If these don't get you into shape, nothing will."

The bodyguard stood by as Sweetikins groomed me. Apparently a Yorkshire Terrier giving a Springer Spaniel a makeover was nothing out of the ordinary for him.

Sweetikins finished and looked me up and down. "You're not bad, for a stalker."

"I'm a Springer…" I began, but was interrupted by a megaphone.

"Ladies and gentleman, the Dog Show is about to start!"

Chapter 10

"What are we going to do about Brutus?" I asked as we trotted towards the car park.

Sweetikins nodded to where Brutus's owner was patting Brutus's mouth with an ice pack. "He's hurt his teeth dragging that heavy table. Shame."

Just then I smelt my favourite smell in the whole world. Mike!

"Nearly chickened out myself," he said, clipping on my lead. "Doesn't look like *she's* pleased to see me here after all." He glanced at Brutus's owner who glared back. "Maybe it wasn't a kiss in that letter. Maybe she was crossing something out."

I felt guilty but there was no time to dwell on Mike's love life. We joined the circle of dogs and owners as Tamsin Parker-Smetherington tottered towards us, holding Sweetikins who was now wearing a sequin-covered bikini and tiara.

"Sweety and I will be judging 'Best in Show'. Good luck everybody, and let the Dog Show begin!" She blew a kiss to the crowd and Mike dropped his programme in excitement.

Over on the grass bank, Brutus let out a whimper.

★★★

"And finally, the winner of 'Dog Most Like Its Owner' is... Scruffy!" the judge announced. "Would all our winners please enter the show ring where Tamsin will choose 'Best in Show'."

I led Mike proudly back into the centre of the car park. This time there had been no big disasters, and we had won 'Dog With The Most Beautiful Eyes' again.

As we stood waiting for Tamsin to choose the overall winner, I couldn't help worrying. What if Mike squashed the cup again? What if he head-butted Tamsin? His hand was trembling so much that my lead was shaking. I licked his hand reassuringly.

Mike dropped the lead. He crouched to pick it up just as Tamsin bent to stroke me.

"I can see why you won 'Most Beautiful Eyes'," she said.

All my beautiful eyes wanted to do was look at Mike and make sure he wasn't going to stand up and head-butt Tamsin in the face. History was going to repeat itself. I had to stop Mike from standing up, but how?

"And so well behaved too!" Tamsin continued.

With a yap, I hurled myself at Mike. Together we tumbled to the ground.

"Thanks, Maddy," Mike muttered, standing up and brushing himself down.

My tail drooped as I watched Tamsin swiftly moving

on to the next dog. We'd blown it.

"The 'Best in Show' cup, and a pack of Sweetikins's new range of grooming products, goes to... Lulu!"

Lula was a little Cocker Spaniel and the winner of the 'Most Adorable Puppy' class. She bounced up and down as her owner led her to Tamsin to receive the cup, which I noticed still had a few dents.

Mike patted me. "Never mind, Maddy. Let's leave it to the youngsters, eh?"

"Before you go, I have a special prize to announce," Tamsin continued. "'The Dog The Judge's Dog Would Most Like To Take Home'." She lifted Sweetikins out of her handbag. "Choose the winner, Sweety!"

Sweetikins trotted towards me, wagging her tail.

It wasn't just Mike's legs that were trembling as he led me towards Tamsin—it was mine too!

"Here is your prize—a bottle of the new dog perfume *Simply Sweetikins*!"

Tamsin handed over a sparkly scent bottle to Mike.

He fumbled with it and dropped it. It fell through the air, spinning. I leapt forward and caught it in my teeth. Everyone sighed with relief.

"Thank you, Tamsin," Mike stammered as I gave it back to him. "I'll wear it always."

Tamsin gave him a funny look, tucked Sweetikins into her bag and hurried away.

"See you at my next star appearance!" Sweetikins called.

I wagged goodbye, then gave Mike a pull. It was time to take him home.

Chapter 11

"Happy now?" Hamlet asked later that evening. He was lying on the tumble drier doing a crossword. Writing that letter had opened up a whole new world for him.

"I suppose," I said, toying with a rawhide chew Mike had given me as a reward.

"You smell terrible, by the way."

"I smell like a celebrity. This is *Simply Sweetikins.*"

"Simply Disgusting, if you ask me."

"It is, isn't it? I'll go and roll in some mud tomorrow." The thought cheered me up and I settled down in my basket to review the day.

"What begins with 's', has six letters and means

'mystery'?" Hamlet asked.

I wasn't listening. "I quite enjoyed all that. Sniffing out clues, following trails. Maybe I could do it again—be a detective. I could call myself 'The Nose', only that was Brutus's idea."

"Secret!" Hamlet exclaimed, scribbling down his answer.

"Yes! Secret Spaniel. I'll put an advert on the dog toilet, get a few clients, solve some mysteries, and who knows? Maybe I'll be as famous as Sweetikins."

"You're certainly as smelly as her."

I ignored him. "I'll lend you a paw with the ironing tomorrow. Night night."

Life was good.

Discussion Points

1. Who asked Maddy to find out who the mystery dog was?

2. Where was Sweetikins when Maddy found her in London?

a) At a clothes shop

b) At a bookshop

c) At a train station

3. What was your favourite part of the story?

4. What category did Maddy win at the Dog Show?

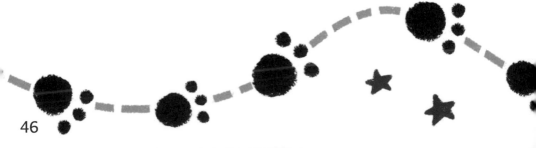

5. Why do you think Brutus wanted Maddy to stop Sweetikins?

6. Who was your favourite character and why?

7. There were moments in the story when Maddy had to **think quickly**. Where do you think the story shows this most?

8. What do you think happens after the end of the story?

Book Bands for Guided Reading

The Institute of Education book banding system is a scale of colours that reflects the various levels of reading difficulty. The bands are assigned by taking into account the content, the language style, the layout and phonics. Word, phrase and sentence level work is also taken into consideration.

The Maverick Readers Scheme is a bright, attractive range of books covering the pink to grey bands. All of these books have been book banded for guided reading to the industry standard and edited by a leading educational consultant.

To view the whole Maverick Readers scheme, visit our website at

www.maverickearlyreaders.com

Or scan the QR code to view our scheme instantly!

Maverick Chapter Readers
(From Lime to Grey Band)